Lucy's Mask

Lisa Sirkis Thompson

Illustrations by John Thompson

To all the workers in masks
who keep us healthy and safe.

First paperback edition May, 2020
ISBN: 979-8-6461-9333-0

www.ohbessie.com

There's
nothing to do.

I can't even
see my friends.

There's nobody
in the whole
wide world to
play with.

I love masks!

With a mask...

...I can be whatever I want.
And nobody will know it's me.

I can be a detective!

I will solve a mystery.

I will search for hidden clues.

or...

I can be an explorer!

I will discover rare bugs.

I will hunt for lost cities

or...

I can be a pirate!

With a secret map.

I will find buried treasure.

or...

I can be a queen!

I will be kind to all my loyal subjects.

I will save them from fire breathing dragons.

or...

I can be a superhero!

I will save the world!

I've been calling you.
I finished your mask.

This is a special kind of mask.
Let's try it on.

NOW you're a superhero!
With this kind of mask you really
will help save the world!

CPSIA information can be obtained
at www.ICGtesting.com
Printed in the USA
LVHW072305241020
669623LV00002B/4

* 9 7 9 8 6 4 6 1 9 3 3 3 0 *